Julie Danneberg & Margot Apple

Cowboy Slim

Charlesbridge

To Jack: Thanks for being my "in-house" editor!—J. D.

For Baxter Black—M. A.

Published by Charlesbridge
85 Main Street
Watertown, MA 02472
(617) 926-0329
www.charlesbridge.com

Library of Congress Cataloging-in-Publication Data
Danneberg, Julie, 1958–
    Cowboy Slim / Julie Danneberg ; illustrated by Margot Apple.
        p. cm.
    Summary: Untalented at riding, roping, and cracking a whip, Slim the cowboy calms a stampeding herd of cattle with his poetry.
    ISBN-13: 978-1-58089-045-8; ISBN-10: 1-58089-045-8 (reinforced for library use)
[1. Cowboys—Fiction. 2. Poetry—Fiction.] I. Apple, Margot, ill. II. Title.
PZ7.D2327Co 2005
[E]—dc22   2004018937

Printed in China
(hc) 10 9 8 7 6 5 4 3 2 1

Illustrations done in watercolor and pencil on Arches paper
Type set in Clarendon
Color separations by Chroma Graphics, Singapore
Printed and bound by Jade Productions
Production supervision by Brian G. Walker
Designed by Susan Mallory Sherman

"I've always wanted to be a real cowboy!" Slim confessed to the other ranch hands on his first day of work at the WJ Ranch.

Slim loved bein' a cowboy. He loved the way his boots kicked up the scent of silver green sage. He loved the way a newborn calf looked at him with long-lashed, velvet brown eyes. He especially loved sittin' by the flickerin' fire and savorin' the smoky taste of pork 'n' beans.

At night back in the bunkhouse, while the other cowboys slept, Slim wrote poems about what he loved. He couldn't help it. He thought about his day, and pretty soon the words tumbled out, one after the other across the paper, like puppies playin' in the yard.

Sometimes just before turnin' in,
he'd saunter outside to recite under the dark,
blue-flannel sky. And as he spoke, with words as soft and warm
as a broken-in quilt, the cows stopped a-snortin' and mooin' in the
corral. The horses stopped a-stompin' and neighin' in the field. And
the lonely coyote on the hill stopped howlin' in the middle of its song.

Moon's silver soft shimmer
Chases shadows away.
Stars shine and glimmer,
A twinkling bouquet.

Wind whispers through treetops,
A low whooshing song.
"Hush, hush," says the river
As it rushes along.

"Goodnight," calls the hoot owl
Perched in the tree.
"Sleep tight," calls the darkness
Wrapped tight around me.

One mornin' the cowboys found a stack of Slim's poems peekin' out from under his bedroll. They got to actin' all frothy, lookin' like they'd been raised on sour milk.

"Real cowboys whip those dogies into shape. They don't mess around with no fancy, perfumed words," blustered Buster as he flicked a fly off the windowsill with his whip.

"Real cowboys ride better than they walk.
They don't write better than they talk," exclaimed
Sally as she fed her horse, Buttermilk, a carrot.

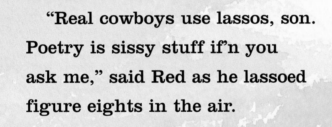

"Real cowboys use lassos, son.
Poetry is sissy stuff if'n you
ask me," said Red as he lassoed
figure eights in the air.

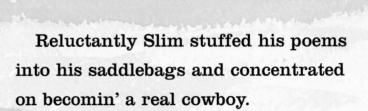

Reluctantly Slim stuffed his poems
into his saddlebags and concentrated
on becomin' a real cowboy.

One mornin' Red met Slim at the door of the bunkhouse. "Jingle your spurs, pardner. We're takin' a herd of cattle to Dodge City."

While the cowboys burned the breeze toward the corral, Slim tried to saddle the git-up end of his horse.

Buster snapped his bullwhip in the air until the herd lunged and lurched ahead like a steam engine pullin' away from the station.

Sally threaded Buttermilk in and out of the tangled mess of cattle, weavin' them into a single herd.

And Red, his lasso formin' a rawhide halo above his head, sent that loop a-whizzin' through the air and landed it snug around the corral gate. "Move 'em out," Red yipped and yee-hawed as he welcomed the herd onto the far-reachin' range.

"Wait for me," yelled Slim just before his horse dumped him to the ground.

"Cain't, buckeroo," said Red.

"Only real cowboys ride in front," said Sally.

"You'll have to ride caboose, son," said Buster with a smile.

The land stretches out
Till it touches the sky.
A whippoorwill sings.
A raven flies by.

So Slim took his place in the billowin' cloud of trail dust at the back of the herd. And although the dust stung his eyes and the whittle-whangin' of the bawlin' cattle tried his patience, the clip-clop rhythm of the ride started tappin' itself into a poem in Slim's mind.

Suddenly, out of the corner of his eye, Slim spied a calf trapped in a narrow ravine. Grabbin' his lasso, he said, "Here's my chance to be a real cowboy."

It wasn't.

As the river of cattle snaked and slithered its way past the red-tinged cliffs, the desert colors painted themselves into a poem in Slim's mind.

Thunderclouds distant
Rumble with rain.
Crickets start creaking.
A noontime refrain.

Without warnin' a heifer decided to go that-a-way even though the herd was a-headin' this-a-way.

"I can surely take care of this myself," Slim said.

He couldn't.

After lunch the scorchin' sun heated up the plains hotter than a chuck wagon's cookstove. "If'n we don't get these hot dogies a-movin', they'll be roasted alive," said Buster.

Slim rode toward the herd, a-hootin' and a-hollerin', wavin' his Stetson with one hand and flappin' his bandanna with the other.

The cattle never even looked up.

"I'm as out of place as a bull in a china shop," Slim said
to himself. "I best be leavin' this work to the real McCoy."
He turned his horse and hit the flats for home, ridin' away
from the herd and his dream.

As Slim rode off into the horizon, the afternoon do-si-doed by, and thunderclouds piled high in the hazy blue distance. A hush fell over the range, and a zing of electricity filled the air. The cattle snorted nervously. Sally, Buster, and Red tightened their grips on their reins. All of a sudden, a clap of thunder echoed off the canyon walls.

A flash of lightnin' tore through the gray curtain of clouds.

Red roped.

Buster whipped.

Sally galloped.

But no matter what those crusty cowboys did, their cranky cattle
kept headin' full speed toward the edge of Deadman's Canyon.

In no time flat, the herd caught up to Slim, sweepin' him
along like a feather in the wind. Huggin' rawhide, he bent over
his horse's neck. To calm his own fears, Slim began a-talkin',
his voice as warm as spring-pure sunshine and as sweet as
new prairie grass.

And as he spoke, the riled-up cattle runnin' right next to
him got sorta curious. Prickin' up their ears, they slowed just a
little and strained to listen.

Slim noticed the change in the herd. He started beltin' out words as clear and refreshin' as a high mountain stream.

Lightning and thunder
Won't put you under.
No need to fear.
This cowboy is near.

Gosh darn it if even more of those spooked cattle didn't cool their heels! They stopped twitchin' and a-quiverin' and put on the brakes.

Boomin' out his poems louder than an afternoon thunder guster, Slim kept on rainin' words as he skidded to a stop right at the very edge of the cliff.

The cattle stopped, too.

Coyotes might howl.
At night they will prowl.
No need to fear.
This cowboy is near.

Slim took a deep breath, his heart chuggin' faster than a runaway locomotive. The other cowboys arrived in a cloud of dust.

"Why, Slim," they called out in a cowboy chorus, "you saved the herd!"

Slim brushed the dust off his chaps and wiped his forehead. "Don't matter none," he said. "I still cain't rope, whip, or ride."

"Dagnabbit, Slim, you done lassoed that herd with yer words!" Red said.

"You sure 'nuff whipped those dogies into shape," agreed Buster.

"And your ridin' wasn't half bad, son," said Sally.

Slim ruminated on their words for what seemed like a long while. Then his face broke out in a grin as wide as the Rio Grande.

"Well, ain't that a dinger! I guess I'm more than a catalog cowboy after all!"

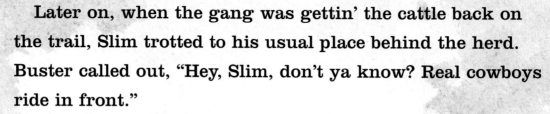

Later on, when the gang was gettin' the cattle back on the trail, Slim trotted to his usual place behind the herd. Buster called out, "Hey, Slim, don't ya know? Real cowboys ride in front."

And as they rode off into the sunset, Slim said, "Hey, Red, how about a lasso lesson?"

"Plenty a-time for that later, amigo," Red said. "Right now I need a word that rhymes with dogies."

Author's Note

Cowboy poets like Slim really do exist. Their tradition of storytelling and song began during the long-ago days of the trail drive and the wide-open range. Composed during long hours in the saddle, stories and songs provided nighttime entertainment around the flickering campfire as well as a calming lullaby to the restless herd. Eventually this oral tradition of words and song evolved into poetry.

Buckaroo Banter

Ain't that a dinger?: Isn't that a big surprise?

burned the breeze: rode really fast

catalog cowboy: a cowboy who is so new that his clothes look like they just came out of a catalog

dogie: a motherless calf in a range herd

frothy: all worked up and angry

git-up end of a horse: rear end of a horse

huggin' rawhide: sticking to the saddle while riding a wild or fast horse

jingle your spurs: hurry up

whittle-whangin': quarreling